D1362420

LOVE TO READ Books, PO Box 621552, Littleton, CO 80162 USA
(800) 216-6649
Printed in the U.S.A.
Library of Congress Catalog Card Number: 98-91584
ISBN 0-9665222-5-7
First Printing 1999

God bless all the children.

Sweet Dreams
Christie and Summer

LOVE TO READ

Books

The Pond Story

BY BARBIE MARSH

Illustrations by Kathy Kniss

There were trees, oh so many trees. Green trees, orange trees, blue trees, yellow trees, aqua trees, and red trees surrounded oh so many friends on the pond.

Tom thunked out of the sparkling pond and trudged by the tallest yellow tree. He felt a crack, a smack, and then a plunk on his back.

It was Cheek, Peek, Sneak, and Meek. "Che, che, che, che," chattered those playful, bushytailed squirrels as they pelted Tom with acorns.

Tom gazed up and grinned at his friends. They raced down the tree to play.

It was warm and a breeze whispered through those trees and rippled across the peaceful pond. The water was blue, no big waves, quiet and beautiful. The fish did flip flops as they jumped at delicious mosquitos.

Ace was out skywriting over the pond. As he flew, he painted the letters G and R and I and Z in bright colors.

Tom asked Cheek, Peek, Sneak, and Meek, "Can you read the word on the pond?" They chattered about it like squirrels do, but had no idea what it said. After tossing and catching some acorns, they decided to go with Tom to the other side of the pond to ask wise old Tuff.

Henrietta poked her big floppy ears and pink nose out of her rabbit hole. Her two big feet went hop hoppity hop hop toward the pond. They were skipping hops because she was a rabbit who loved to dance and play. Tom asked Henrietta, "Do you know what G–R–I–Z spells?"

Henrietta twitched her nose, flopped her ears, and fluffed her tail, but just couldn't figure it out. So off they went. Cheek, Peek, Sneak, and Meek scurried around. Tom thunked along thoughtfully. Henrietta hopped ahead.

Flutter, the swallowtail butterfly, lifted her wings above Tom. She was curious about the new word and eager to fly along with her friends.

Tom lifted his long neck. "Listen to Old Blue and Betsy." He heard another loud TWEET TWEET TWEET TWEET. It was not their usual soft tweet tweet twa twa tweet. Tom listened to the birds, heard warning in their notes, and stepped fast – for a turtle that is.

Then crackle, crunch, crackle went the leaves. Tom, Flutter, Cheek, Peek, Sneak, Meek, and Henrietta stopped in their tracks. Out of the tall grass tiptoed a graceful, young fawn.

"What is your name?" asked Tom. "My name is Doe. May I join your hike?" Tom smiled a big yes and off they went together.

Doe pranced. Tom thunked. Henrietta hopped. Flutter floated. Cheek, Peek, Sneak, and Meek scurried by Old Blue and Betsy's tall tree. These two cheerful bluebirds lived in a nest high above the quiet pond in a white tree and loved to chirp together.

The season was summer. The breeze over the pond was warm. Some fresh flowers sweetened the air around Tuff's red tree. Tuff moved his tall brown wing away from his face and gazed down from his high branch. As he woke up he stretched, yawned, and exhaled a friendly, "Whoo Whoo Whoo are you?" Tom smiled at his old wise friend and cheerfully greeted him. All of the friends were eager to discover what G–R–I–Z spells.

Then without warning a large, brown, hungry bear came growling out of the trees. The grizzly bear's face was fierce. "The word that Ace tried to warn you about," hooted Tuff, "spells Griz!"

Henrietta hopped faster than usual and jumped into a friend's rabbit hole. Cheek, Peek, Sneak, and Meek scurried up the nearest tree. Doe raced at her swiftest speed through the thicket and hid in the tall grass with her family. Old Blue and Betsy were silent.

Tom swam at a turtle's pace over to his rock. It was green just like his shell, and so the perfect camouflage. Tom pulled both arms into his shell, then both legs, his tail and his head. He looked just like another rock. It was silent on the pond.

Griz threw his strong arm into the pond and scooped
up a fish with his sharp claws. Lumbering, splashing, and
scooping up fish, Griz made his way toward Tom's rock.
He stood up on his great legs and let out a fierce
"GRRRRRRRRRR!" Tom shook in his shell.

Griz scooped up some more fish
and then at record lumbering speed he
splashed his way to shore, ran on all fours,
and disappeared behind the trees.

Tuff hooted a friendly, "Whoo!
Whoo! Whoo! Griz is gone." Ace
flew out over the pond spelling three
words in bright colors.
GOOD NIGHT FRIENDS!
Old Blue and Betsy tweeted their
favorite nighttime lullaby.

Cheek, Peek, Sneak, and Meek danced back to their nest in the yellow tree.

Tom poked his head out of his shell and smiled. It was dark except for the bright moon over the pond. It was a peaceful pond and the fish were jumping again.

There were trees, oh so many trees. Green trees,
orange trees, blue trees, yellow trees, aqua trees, and red
trees surrounded oh so many friends on the pond.